THE PRINCESS AND THE PEA

RACHEL ISADORA

G. P. PUTNAM'S SONS

Once upon a time,
there was a prince.

THE PRINCESS AND THE PEA

RACHEL ISADORA

G. P. PUTNAM'S SONS

Once upon a time,
there was a prince.

The prince wanted to marry
a real princess, so he traveled all
over the world in the hopes of
finding such a lady.

He met many princesses,
but it was difficult to tell
whether they were real ones.

ISKA WARAN

There was something about each
princess that was not quite right,
so the prince came home again
and was sad.

One evening, there was a terrible storm. Suddenly a knocking was heard at the gate, and the old king went to open it.

There was a princess
standing at the gate.
But, good gracious!
What a sight the rain
and the wind had
made her look.
   And yet she
said she was a real
princess.

"Ah! We shall soon find out if she is real," said the Queen. So she went into the bedroom, where she laid a pea upon the bedstead. Then she took twenty mattresses and laid them on the pea, and then put twenty feather beds on top of the mattresses.

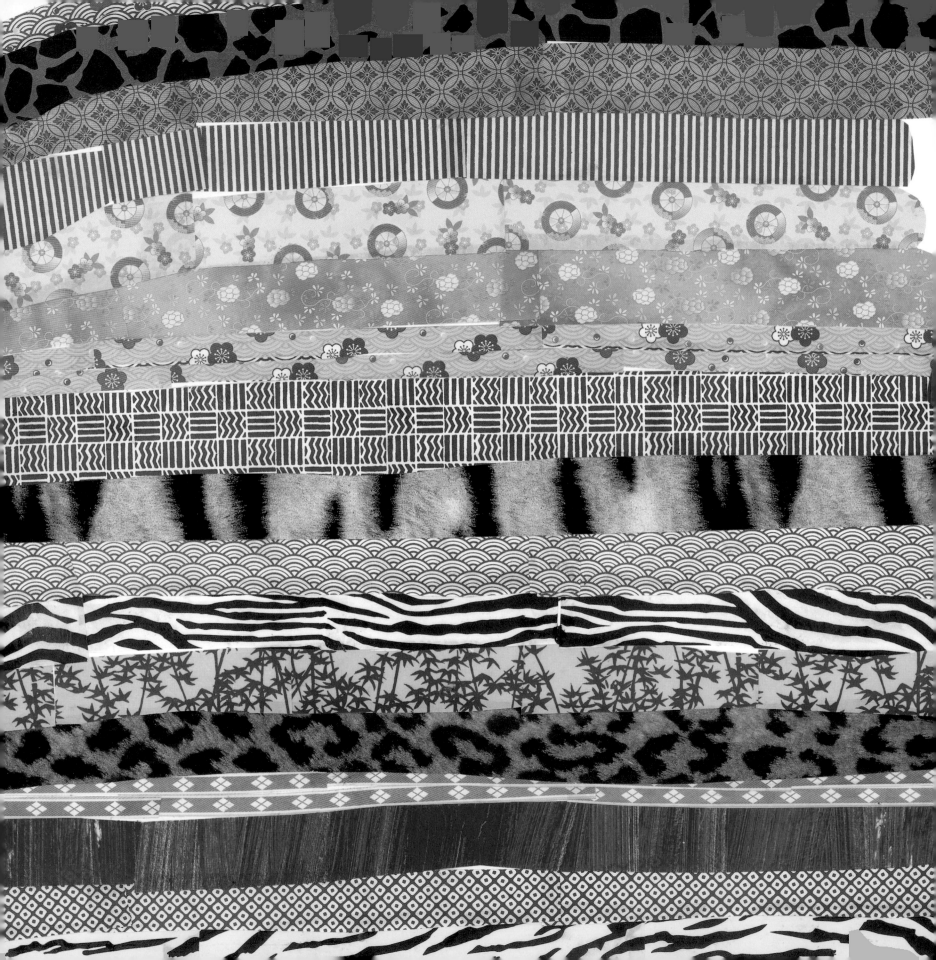

On this the princess had to lie all night.

The next morning, the princess was asked how she had slept.

"Oh, very badly!" said the princess. "I scarcely closed my eyes all night. Heaven only knows what was in the bed, but I was lying on something hard, so that I am black and blue all over."

"That's horrible!" said the king.

Now they knew that she was a real princess because she had felt the pea right through the twenty mattresses and the twenty feather beds.

Nobody but a real princess could be as sensitive as that.

So the prince took the princess
for his wife.

The pea was put in
a museum, where it
may still be seen,
if no one has stolen it.

There, that is a true story.

THREE WAYS TO SAY HELLO IN AFRICA

Ethiopia — **SELAM** (Amharic)

Somalia — **ISKA WARAN** (Somali)

Kenya — **JAMBO, HABARI** (Swahili)

To John and Hildegard

G. P. PUTNAM'S SONS A division of Penguin Young Readers Group. Published by The Penguin Group. Penguin Group (USA) Inc., 375 Hudson Street, New York, NY 10014, U.S.A. Penguin Group (Canada), 90 Eglinton Avenue East, Suite 700, Toronto, Ontario, Canada M4P 2Y3 (a division of Pearson Penguin Canada Inc.). Penguin Books Ltd, 80 Strand, London WC2R 0RL, England. Penguin Ireland, 25 St. Stephen's Green, Dublin 2, Ireland (a division of Penguin Books Ltd.). Penguin Group (Australia), 250 Camberwell Road, Camberwell, Victoria 3124, Australia (a division of Pearson Australia Group Pty Ltd). Penguin Books India Pvt Ltd, 11 Community Centre, Panchsheel Park, New Delhi - 110 017, India. Penguin Group (NZ), Cnr Airborne and Rosedale Roads, Albany, Auckland 1310, New Zealand (a division of Pearson New Zealand Ltd). Penguin Books (South Africa) (Pty) Ltd, 24 Sturdee Avenue, Rosebank, Johannesburg 2196, South Africa. Penguin Books Ltd, Registered Offices: 80 Strand, London WC2R 0RL, England.

Manufactured in China by South China Printing Co. Ltd. Design by Marikka Tamura. Text set in Geist. The illustrations were done with oil paints, printed paper and palette paper.
Library of Congress Cataloging-in-Publication Data
Isadora, Rachel. The princess and the pea / Rachel Isadora. p. cm.
Summary: A simplified version of the tale in which a girl proves that she is a real princess by feeling a pea through twenty mattresses and twenty featherbeds. [1. Fairy tales.] I. Andersen, H. C. (Hans Christian), 1805–1875. Prindsessen paa ærten. English. II. Title. PZ8.I84Prm 2007 [E]—dc22 2006024712
ISBN 978-0-399-24611-1
2 3 4 5 6 7 8 9 10
FIRST IMPRESSION